Henry and Melinda
Sports Stories

MYSTERY AT THE
BASKETBALL GAME

By Silky Sullivan

Illustrations by Lois Axeman

Φ CHILDRENS PRESS, CHICAGO

Library of Congress Cataloging in Publication Data

Sullivan, Silky.
  Mystery at the basketball game.

  (Henry and Melinda sports stories)
  Summary: Henry makes one mistake after another in the
championship basketball game until Melinda notices that
his feet look funny.
  [1. Basketball—Fiction] I. Axeman, Lois, ill.
II. Title. III. Series: Sullivan, Silky. Henry and
Melinda sports stories.
PZ7.S9537My   [Fic]   81-12252
ISBN 0-516-01921-X   AACR2

Mother and Melinda were going to Henry's
basketball game. They were very excited.

"May I carry your gym shoes?" said Melinda.
"May I, Henry? Please!"

Henry laughed. "You will need a clothespin for your nose." But he gave her the shoes.

They walked to the bus stop together. Mother carried the tickets. Henry carried a bag with his uniform in it. Melinda carried Henry's gym shoes.

"Your shoes are awfully big," said Melinda.

"So are my feet," said Henry.

"If my team wins tonight," said Henry,
"we will get a trophy."

"What's a trophy?" asked Melinda.

"A prize," said Henry, "that means
we are the best team in the city."

Mother was worried. "You did not eat
enough supper," she said.

"I was just too nervous to eat," said
Henry.

"Why are you nervous?" asked Melinda.

"I am the tallest player on the team," said Henry. "Everyone expects me to get the ball. After I get the ball, they expect me to score."

"You do that all the time," said Melinda.

"This team is really tough," said Henry.
"They will play two men against me for sure."

"That's not fair," said Melinda.

"When you are the tallest player, they
think it's fair," said Henry.

Henry started to the locker room.

"Wait!" said Mother. "Don't forget your
uniform." He came back for his uniform.

"Wait!" said Melinda. "Don't forget
your shoes!" He came back for his shoes.
"How can I play ball?" he asked. "I
can't even think straight!"
Mother gave him a kiss. "Don't be
nervous, dear. We will cheer for you."

Mother and Melinda sat in the stands. Everyone ate hot dogs and popcorn. They yelled Henry's name over and over again.

Melinda asked, "Why are they yelling
at Henry?"

"Henry is their hero," said Mother.
"They expect him to win the game."

Melinda put down her popcorn. "I think
I'm nervous," she said.

The game began.

Right away, Henry got the ball. The crowd cheered. He bounced the ball off his foot. The crowd booed.

"Mother," said Melinda, "Henry's feet look funny."

"They do not," said Mother. "He has lovely feet."

Henry got the ball again. The crowd
cheered. He bounced the ball off his
other foot. The crowd booed.

"Mother," said Melinda, "Henry's feet
look funny!"

"Be nice," said Mother, "or I will
make you leave."

Henry got the ball again. The crowd cheered. He tripped over his own feet! The crowd booed even louder. "Take him out! Take him out!" they cried.

"Mother," said Melinda, "Henry's feet—!"

"Not another word," said Mother.
"Your poor brother!"

Henry's coach took him out of the game.
Poor Henry was so unhappy.

"Mother," said Melinda, "I am going to look at Henry's feet."

She crept down to the players' bench. His feet *did* look funny.

"Henry!" she whispered. "Your shoes
are on the wrong feet!"

Henry looked surprised. Then he looked happy. "Hey, coach," he said, "I was so nervous I put my shoes on the wrong feet!"

The coach looked surprised and happy, too. "Well, change them around," he said.

Henry changed his shoes around. He went
back into the game. He got the ball. He
faked, he dribbled, he scored.
The crowd went wild.

Henry's team won the trophy. They were
very happy. They acted silly and posed
for pictures.

The coach said, "We won this game because of Henry's little sister. Melinda was the only one who knew that his shoes were on the wrong feet."

They gave Melinda a small trophy of her very own. Henry carried her around the gym on his shoulders. Everyone cheered for Henry and Melinda.

UNFAMILIAR WORDS
(based on the Spache Readability Formula)

Most of the following unfamiliar words in *Mystery at the Basketball Game* are made clear through the illustrations and content.

awfully	everyone	popcorn
basketball	expect	posed
bench	expects	score
booed	faked	scored
bounced	foot	shoulders
cheer	gym	tickets
cheered	hero	tonight
clothespin	hey	tough
coach	kiss	trophy
crept	locker	uniform
crowd	nervous	wild
dribbled	players'	won

About the Author

Silky Sullivan is a Phi Beta Kappa graduate of the University of Michigan and a children's librarian who resides in Royal Oak, Michigan, with her artist husband and their tailless cat. The Henry and Melinda stories were inspired by her husband, who, at age fifteen, began teaching his younger sister, then three, to play basketball. His sister went on to become a superstar and very successful coach. Says Ms. Sullivan, "The whole family loves sports. We're all athletic. I'm writing from experience."

About the Artist

Lois Axeman is a native Chicagoan who lives with her Shih-tzu dog, Marty, in a sunny, plant-filled highrise overlooking a large Chicago park. Marty accompanies Lois to and from her studio in town. After attending the American Academy and the Institute of Design (IIT), Lois started as a fashion illustrator in a department store. When the children's wear illustrator became ill, Lois took her place and found that she loved drawing children. She started freelancing then, and has been doing text and picture books ever since. Lois teaches classes on illustration at the University of Illinois, Circle Campus.